Science, Maker, and Real Technology Students

S.M.A.R.T.S.

S.M.A.R.T.S. is published by Stone Arch Books
A Capstone Imprint
1710 Roe Crest Drive
North Mankato, MN 56003
www.capstonepub.com

Text and illustrations © 2016 Stone Arch Books

Library of Congress Cataloging-in-Publication Data is available on the Library
of Congress website.

ISBN: 978-1-4965-0466-1 (hardcover) 978-1-4965-0474-6 (paperback) 978-
1-4965-2343-3 (eBook PDF)

Summary: Hubble Middle School is getting some strange visitors — a UFO
has been spotted hovering around the school in what could be a monumental
first encounter. But is it for real? It's up to the S.M.A.R.T.S.
to separate fact from fiction in this paranormal puzzler.

Designer: Hilary Wacholz

Printed in China by Nordica
0416/CA21600331
022016   009563R

S.M.A.R.T.S.

AND THE MISSING UFO

By Melinda Metz

Illustrated by Heath McKenzie

STONE ARCH BOOKS
a capstone imprint

1

"How are you feeling about your face-off against the Mad Scientists next week?" Mrs. Ram — short for Mrs. Ramanujan — asked the S.M.A.R.T.S. kids Thursday afternoon. They were all gathered in the makerspace in Hubble Middle School's media center. That's where the S.M.A.R.T.S. — also known as Science, Maker, and Real Technology Students — always met. Mrs. Ram was the club's sponsor as well as the school's fifth-grade science teacher.

"We still haven't figured out what mystery to solve," Zoe Branson admitted.

"It's going to end in DOOM!" Caleb Quinn exclaimed. "We're not ready at all."

"Doom might be an exaggeration," Jaden Thompson said, "but we *are* having a hard time deciding what to do."

Zoe, Caleb, and Jaden had gone to school together since kindergarten, but it wasn't until they'd joined S.M.A.R.T.S. at the beginning of the year that they'd realized how much they had in common — namely a love of science. Now they were all great friends.

"Well, it sounds like your goal for today's S.M.A.R.T.S. meeting should be to figure out which real-life mystery to tackle," Mrs. Ram said. "You have less than a week until we face off against the Mad Scientists."

Zoe, Caleb, and Jaden exchanged worried glances. The two clubs were having a competition to see who could use their science skills to come up with the best solution to a real-life mystery. And the Mad Scientists, the science club at nearby Edison Middle School, were supposed to be really smart.

"I'll be in Mr. Leavey's office if you need me," Mrs. Ram continued. "We need to finish up the arrangements for tomorrow afternoon's get-together." She and Mr. Leavey, the media center librarian, had invited the Mad Scientists to Hubble Middle School so the members of both clubs could meet each other before the competition.

"The Mad Scientists are the enemy," Caleb muttered once Mrs. Ram was out of earshot. "I don't need to sit around eating cookies with them."

"I say cookies are good any time," Sonja, one of the other S.M.A.R.T.S. kids, said.

"We have more important things to talk about than cookies," Jaden said. "Mrs. Ram is right. We have to decide on what mystery we're going to solve. We're already running out of time, and we haven't even gotten started yet."

Caleb pressed his hands against his head. "DOOM," he muttered. "I knew it."

Zoe tried to calculate how many times Caleb used the word *DOOM* in the average day. It had to be more than twenty. Caleb always thought something disastrous was about to happen, and Zoe and Jaden were always trying to convince him he was wrong.

"We still have time," Zoe told Caleb. "We just have to make a choice. And whatever it is has to be fabulous."

"The Loch Ness Monster —" Benjamin, another of the S.M.A.R.TS., began.

"— is the best choice," Samuel, his twin brother, finished for him. The twins were always finishing each other's sentences. They also dressed and looked exactly alike, hence their nicknames — Thing One and Thing Two.

"But that mystery's already been solved," Goo, whose real name was actually Maya, said. She'd earned her nickname because she could come up with info faster than Google. She remembered everything she'd ever read.

"It has?" Caleb asked.

Goo nodded. "A geologist figured out that Loch Ness Monster sightings happened most often when there was seismic activity. There's a fault line under the lake, and earthquakes make the surface bubble. That's what people who claim they've seen Nessie have actually seen."

"But what about the picture that shows the head and the long neck? The one that looks like a plesiosaur coming out of the water?" Caleb asked.

"I read about that too," Goo said. "It wasn't even taken in Scotland. It's actually a picture of an elephant coming out of the water in Sri Lanka. Or at least that's what the person who wrote the article thought."

"Even if we wanted to investigate Nessie, we can't go to Scotland," Jaden said. "I wish we could. I heard something really cool always follows the Loch Ness Monster around."

"What?" Sonja asked.

"A really, really, really big tail," Jaden said, then laughed.

"You've reached your limit," Zoe informed him. She only allowed Jaden to make three of his bad jokes a day, at least in her presence. He'd already made a complete stinker that morning before school and another one almost as bad at lunch.

"How about the mystery of the Abominable Snowman?" Dylan suggested.

"We can't go to the Himalayas either," Jaden said, resisting the impulse to tell an Abominable Snowman joke. He needed to keep focused. They all did. They couldn't let the Mad Scientists win the contest. "What else?"

"What about ghosts?" Sonja suggested from the table she shared with Goo. "Ghosts are everywhere."

"Ghosts would be cool," Zoe agreed. "But how do we get one to appear?"

As soon as the words left her mouth, a whining sound filled the room. It oscillated from high to low and made her ears throb.

"What's that?" Caleb yelled.

Benjamin and Samuel each raised an arm. In unison, they pointed toward the window, their eyes wide with fear.

Caleb jerked his head toward it. A wide circle of lights hovered in the gray October sky. The formation wasn't like anything he'd ever seen. He had to swallow once, twice, three times before he could speak. "UFO!" he hollered.

2

"Alien attack!" Caleb shouted, diving under his table.

Dylan grabbed his bike helmet out of his backpack and strapped it on, then added a pair of safety goggles from his workstation.

"We need weapons!" Sonja snatched up the closest thing within reach — a tape measure — then threw it back down in disgust.

"Run in a zigzag pattern! It'll make it harder for a tractor beam to suck you into the spacecraft!" Antonio hollered, taking off toward the closest row of bookshelves, then lurching left and racing toward the back of the room.

"This is no time to run and cower!" Zoe yelled. "We have to get pictures!" She leaped to her feet and grabbed her cell phone from her backpack.

"She's right!" Jaden called. "We're scientists! We need evidence!"

Zoe raced toward the door, the other kids hot on her heels. Suddenly she spun back around. "Jaden!"

Because of his cerebral palsy, Jaden needed braces to walk. They made him slower than the others. But given that this was an emergency, he didn't seem to mind the other kids racing ahead.

"Go!" Jaden ordered. "I'll catch up."

Zoe nodded, then raced out of the media center, down the hall, and out the front door of the school after everyone else. The UFO was still there. For a moment, all Zoe could do was stare at it. Then she started taking pictures as fast as she could.

"I think it's landing!" Caleb shouted. The eight globes of lights that formed the circle were slowly descending toward the meadow that lay just beyond the school grounds. In moments, the UFO would be out of sight. The group took off again, running alongside the school building.

Zoe turned the corner first. The meadow was empty. So was the sky. "It vanished," she said. "It's just . . . gone."

"Look! By the trees!" Goo shouted, pointing to the woods that bordered the clearing. "Are those aliens?"

Caleb squinted into the darkness of the late October afternoon. He could just make out shadowy figures

disappearing between the trees. A shiver rippled through his body.

"There was definitely someone — or something — moving out there," Caleb hollered. "Anybody get any pictures of them before they got into the woods?"

"Didn't have time," Zoe answered. She bounced from foot to foot, not sure if she wanted to chase after them or run away. "But I definitely got some of the spaceship."

"Well, I think I know what real-life mystery we should solve for the contest," Jaden announced, joining the group. "What's a better mystery than a UFO?"

"You're right. There's no way the Mad Scientists will come up with something cooler," Caleb agreed, still staring out at the dark woods. "We actually saw a UFO. We have to investigate."

Zoe glanced at Caleb, surprised he wasn't coming up with a hundred doom-filled scenarios that could happen if they went charging after aliens. But she didn't blame him for being excited. If there were aliens from another planet right here in town, she wanted to see them. Any science nerd would.

"Should we go after them? I'm not sure we could catch them. They were moving really fast," Antonio said.

"Maybe they teleported," Caleb suggested. "That could explain how quickly they vanished."

"As much as I'd love to investigate now, it's getting dark fast," Jaden said. "Let's meet here before school tomorrow when it's light. We'll be able see if any evidence was left behind."

"I'm in," Caleb said.

"Me too," Zoe agreed.

Goo sighed, looking disappointed. "I can't. I have a dentist appointment. You'll have to tell me everything."

"Definitely," Zoe promised her. "We'll fill in everyone who can't get here early."

"We should all study up on UFOs tonight," Jaden added. "We have our mystery, but we're still going to have to work hard — and fast — if we want to solve it in time for the competition!"

3

Zoe tapped her pen on her open notebook that night as she tried to remember everything she could about the UFO sighting from earlier. After all, an investigation needed facts.

She decided to make a list of her observations to organize her thoughts. That had always helped her and the rest of the S.M.A.R.T.S. solve mysteries in the past. Zoe closed her eyes briefly, trying to replay the UFO sighting in her mind, and then started to write.

OBSERVATIONS:
- Ring of lights about 700 feet in the air
- Lights flickered a little
- Whining sound before UFO appeared — loud enough to be heard inside school
- Lights descended fast — ten seconds?
- UFO seemed like it was going to land in meadow, but nothing was there
- Multiple beings — aliens? — disappearing into the woods

Suddenly there was a creaking sound a few feet away. Zoe gasped and turned around — her sister, Kylie, stood in her doorway.

"Didn't mean to scare you," Kylie said. "I just need to borrow your window."

It wasn't an unusual request. Kylie was always asking to use Zoe's window, because it looked out at the house next door, where Austin, a senior at Kylie's high school, lived.

"I want to spy on the cute boy too," Zoe said, joining her sister at the window.

A few seconds later, the motion-sensitive lights mounted on Austin's garage flashed on, and they saw him wheeling something up the driveway. It was high, like a hospital gurney, and covered with a lumpy looking tarp. Austin pushed the mystery object into his garage and disappeared from sight.

"Oh, no! He's shutting the door," Kylie wailed. She didn't move away from the window until the security lights timed out, and Austin's driveway went dark again. There were still lights on inside the garage, but Austin had tacked sheets over the small square windows, and all Zoe could see was a shadow moving around.

"What do you think he's doing?" Kylie wondered.

"Maybe that stuff he was pushing is something he's going to use for his Halloween decorations," Zoe answered. The holiday was only a few weeks away, and every year Austin went all out. A couple years back, he'd even rented a smoke machine.

"That makes sense," Kylie answered. "Remember last year when he did all that stuff a few weeks before

Halloween to make it look like werewolves were invading the town?"

Zoe laughed. "Like leaving that torn shirt and tufts of dog hair on the backstop of your school's baseball diamond? That was epic."

"He's really creative," Kylie said, her voice getting all gooey. She headed for the door. "Oh, I almost forgot. Mom wanted me to see if you're done with your homework."

"Working on it now," Zoe answered, patting her notebook. Prepping for the UFO investigation was *almost* like homework. And it was hugely important. Depending on why the aliens were here, it could even be life-saving!

* * *

In his own room, Caleb opened his laptop and did a search for the Red Pines Woods where the aliens had disappeared. He needed to figure out *how* the spacecraft had vanished, and finding out more about the area was a good place to start.

The first few articles he found were about how the number of Northern Wild Monkshood plants in the woods was dwindling. One article in particular stood out — it was all about how a local group called the Flower Power Patrol had formed to protect the endangered Monkshood. The leader of the group was so into protecting the planet that he wouldn't wear anything made of animal or plant material. Everything had to be man-made — recycled if possible.

Unfortunately, nothing Caleb read gave him any ideas about how the spacecraft could have disappeared so fast. But it *had* vanished, so there had to be an explanation.

Caleb started a list of possible methods.

HOW SHIP VANISHED:

- Teleportation
- Cloaking device
- Trapdoor under meadow leading to a secret Alien Parking Space
- Spaceship made of super light metal from alien planet that can be folded like a gum wrapper
- Alien shrinking device that lets alien put ship in his pocket
- Mass hypnosis to make us THINK the ship disappeared
- Ship dropped off aliens, then left at warp speed
- Ship was just a pod that was sucked back up into the Mothership by a tractor beam

Caleb read back over his list. What if there *was* a Mothership up there? What if aliens were observing *him*, making lists of their own? What if the aliens *did* have tractor-beam technology? They could suck him out of the house if they wanted to. What if —

Caleb forced himself to take a couple slow, deep breaths, then he decided to focus on his math homework. Math had rules. Math made sense. He'd bring his list to school in the morning. Better to read it again when it was light out and his friends were nearby.

* * *

Back at his house, Jaden put on his black-and-white checked Sherlock Holmes hat. Sometimes it helped him think better, especially when what he was thinking about was a mystery. And he had a mystery now — a big one.

Usually when he was working on a case, Jaden tried to figure out his suspect's motive first. But this

time he didn't exactly have suspects — he had aliens.
Still, even if he wasn't considering them suspects, he
decided to come up with some potential motives.

Hypothesis: Aliens exist

Possible Motives for Flying Next to School:

• Something in the area vital for survival — food,
fuel??

• Aliens are scientists interested in observing young
humans and decided S.M.A.R.T.S. kids would be
the best.

• Aliens want entertainment and think Hubble
Middle School kids would make a good reality
show?

Jaden looked at his list and sighed. How was he supposed to come up with decent motives for alien behavior? They were *aliens*.

"Hey, boy genius," a voice said from the doorway. "I was wondering if you could identify this object for me?"

Jaden glanced up and saw his dad standing there. "Uh, that would be a garbage bag," Jaden answered, waiting for the punch line. His dad loved jokes as much he did.

"Got it in one guess," Dad said. He shook the big plastic bag a couple times to open it, and it made a loud flapping sound. "If you take a look around your room, I bet you can figure out what to do with it."

"Okay, okay. I'll clean up," Jaden said. He had let his room get pretty messy. His dad gave him a half salute and left.

Jaden decided to start with his desk, since he was already sitting there. He began sorting the jumble of papers and half-finished projects into piles. Keep. Toss.

Keep. Toss. While he sorted, Jaden's brain kept returning to the mystery of the missing UFO. He sure hoped the other S.M.A.R.T.S. kids were coming up with some good ideas tonight, because he didn't feel anywhere close to cracking the case.

4

The next morning, Zoe stood at the edge of the meadow, staring up at the bright blue sky as she waited for the others to arrive. She heard a soft whirring sound behind her and spun around with a squeak. She saw Jaden rolling toward her in his wheelchair. Caleb was walking next to him.

"I thought that noise was the UFO starting up," Zoe confessed.

"Just my chair," Jaden said. Usually he just used his leg braces to walk, but since he needed to move over bumpy terrain that morning, he'd decided to go with the wheels.

"It's hard to believe we saw a UFO yesterday," Zoe said, looking up into the sky again.

"It's even harder to believe it vanished!" Caleb exclaimed. "How did something so big disappear? I made a whole list of possibilities, including a cloaking device. If it's cloaked, maybe it didn't vanish at all. Maybe it's sitting right out there in the middle of the meadow."

"Even if the aliens somehow made the ship invisible, it would still weigh something," Zoe argued. "If it was sitting out there, there would be a smushed-down section of grass. Does that look smushy to you?" She pointed to a spot near the treeline, where the meadow gave way to the woods.

"Yeah, it does," Caleb whispered. His throat went dry again, the same way it had when he'd first seen the UFO. Could the spacecraft really be right there?

"Let's get a closer look," Jaden suggested. He started rolling toward the spot with Zoe and Caleb on his wheels. But before they'd gone far, the rest of the S.M.A.R.T.S. arrived.

"We're —" Benjamin shouted from behind them.

"— here!" Samuel yelled.

"Me and Antonio too," Sonja added.

"We want to check out that section of flattened grass over by the trees," Jaden told them. "Maybe the ship landed there."

"And maybe it's even still there — cloaked," Caleb added. "Keep your eyes down as you walk over. There might be alien tracks."

The group made their way across the meadow, stopping when they reached the flattened grass.

"I thought there was a big circle that had been smushed down," Zoe said. "But it's more like a ring made out of flat circles — eight of them to be exact." She took some pictures.

"Wouldn't the grass be flattened everywhere in the circle if an alien spacecraft had landed on it?" Antonio asked.

"Maybe the spacecraft has landing gear," Jaden offered. "Each of the flat sections could be where a wheel touched the ground."

Zoe knelt down so she could get a better look at one of the flat circles. "These don't look like the right shape for a wheel exactly."

"Maybe spaceships don't have wheels," Sonja suggested. "There are definitely marks on the grass in a circle, right below where we saw the UFO. I say it landed here."

Caleb cautiously stretched out his hand. "Nothing there now," he said. "There goes my theory about a cloaking device."

"There are more flat spots heading from the ring to the woods," Antonio pointed out.

"Alien tracks! It has to be!" Caleb said. "We saw aliens disappearing into the woods."

"We need to collect all the data we can," Jaden said. He reached around and pulled a piece of cord out of his backpack, which was strapped to the back of his wheelchair. "We can use this to measure the circumference of the circle."

"I'll help," Sonja said, grabbing one end of the rope.

"I'll take some video and more pictures," Zoe said.

"Let's follow the alien tracks," Caleb told the twins and Antonio. "Maybe one of them dropped something." They each chose one of the lines and began walking slowly alongside them, staring at the ground.

"It would be so cool if one of them stopped to poop," Antonio said.

"So cool," Caleb agreed. "There's no way the Mad Scientists could top alien poop."

Zoe shook her head. Boys had a warped definition of cool. She finished filming the area where they thought the spacecraft had landed, then headed over to film the alien tracks. If only the aliens had traveled across some soft dirt. That way they'd be able to see what their feet looked like. The grass showed signs that something been running across the meadow, but the tracks didn't look much different than the tracks the boys were making looking for evidence.

"I found something!" Sonja yelled from where she was studying a circular imprint.

Everybody hurried back toward her. Sonja held up something small, flat, and red. It was about the size and shape of a penny, but not perfectly round.

"What is it?" Zoe asked.

"I'm not sure," Sonja answered. "It's smooth . . . and brittle." She broke off a tiny piece of the red substance.

"We need to run some tests on it," Jaden said.

Sonja nodded. "Maybe Mrs. Ram will let us use some of the equipment in her science classroom."

"It's our project, though," Antonio reminded them. "Club sponsors aren't allowed to give us ideas about the mysteries we're solving."

"We won't even mention the UFO to her," Zoe said. "We're S.M.A.R.T.S. That means we're smart enough to figure this out on our own!"

5

"A mystery substance — cool!" Mrs. Ram exclaimed when the S.M.A.R.T.S explained why they wanted to use some of the equipment in her classroom. "What have you observed so far?"

"It's smooth and brittle," Sonja began. "Or at least it was when I first picked it up. Now it seems more bendable."

"Good observations!" Mrs. Ram exclaimed. "Anything else?"

"It's a solid," Zoe volunteered. "At least at room temperature."

"Yes!" Mrs. Ram gave a fist pump. "We haven't had the chance to cover some of the other important properties that can help identify a substance yet. A couple of the key ones are if it is soluble — that means if it will dissolve in water — whether or not it melts, and what type of molecular structure it has."

Jaden looked at the clock — only twenty minutes before the first bell. "Let's split into teams," he suggested. "Who wants to be on Team Molecular Structure with me?"

"I will!" Zoe volunteered.

Mrs. Ram used a razor blade to slice off a thin section of the flat, red, irregularly shaped disk, then handed it to Zoe. She and Jaden headed to the back table where a microscope had been set up. Zoe put the sample on a slide, covered it with a square of thin glass, and placed it on the microscope.

Jaden's heart was pounding as he looked through the eyepiece. He could be examining an alien substance. He used the knobs on the side of the microscope to bring the slide into focus, then straightened up.

"It looks like it's covered with tiny cracks," Jaden called to Mrs. Ram, who was helping Team Melt with the hot plate. It was a special one for science that could be set to specific temperatures.

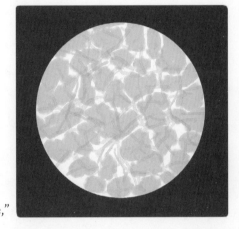

"That means it has what's called a crystalline structure," Mrs. Ram answered. "We can add that to our list of the mystery substance's properties."

"It doesn't dissolve —" Benjamin began.

"— in water," Samuel concluded from the counter by the sink.

"And it's starting to melt," Sonja announced.

"What's the temperature?" Mrs. Ram asked.

"A hundred and fifteen," Antonio said.

Mrs. Ram clapped her hands. "Great. So we have a substance that is solid at room temperature, melts at a hundred and fifteen degrees, is bendable — malleable, in science speak — once it reaches a certain temperature, and has a crystalline structure."

"What are you guys doing in here?" Goo asked, coming into the classroom. She had Mrs. Ram for homeroom, but none of the others did.

"We found something where the —" Zoe stopped. They'd agreed not to even mention the UFO in front of Mrs. Ram. "When we were exploring the meadow. We'll tell you about it later. We're using some of the equipment to figure out what it is."

"Goo! Great! I was just going to Google something," Mrs. Ram said. "Now I can use you. Do you know any substances that have a melting point of a hundred and fifteen degrees Fahrenheit?"

Goo closed her eyes for a moment, thinking. "Different kinds of wax," she said. "Wax melts between 110 and 200 degrees Fahrenheit."

"Awesome!" Mrs. Ram said.

"What else do you know about wax?" Jaden asked. "Is it soluble?"

Goo shook her head. "It won't dissolve in water."

"What kind of molecular structure does it have?" Zoe jumped in.

"Crystalline," Goo answered without hesitating.

"You're awesome, Goo!" Sonja said. "Thanks to you and Mrs. Ram, we know what we found in the meadow is wax."

"What we really need to know is if it's from Earth," Caleb whispered to Zoe and Jaden.

"You guys better get to your own homerooms," Mrs. Ram told them. "Remember to come to the makerspace right after school so you can meet the Mad Scientists."

"They'll be even madder when we beat them," Jaden joked.

6

"What's up with that wax?" Zoe asked her fellow S.M.A.R.T.S. at the lunch table that afternoon. "Is it something the aliens left behind, or is it just a piece of trash that ended up in the meadow?"

"It would be a huge coincidence if we happened to find it right where the aliens parked their ship and it didn't come from them," Jaden answered.

"Why are all of you so sure we saw a spaceship?" Goo asked.

"You were there!" Caleb exclaimed. "You saw it too. A UFO almost right on top of our school."

"Right. A UFO — an Unidentified Flying Object," Goo agreed. "Not a UFS — an Unidentified Flying Saucer. I did some research last night. One article said birds can fly as high as forty thousand feet, *and* they're really reflective. A bird could be a UFO."

"A bird? You think we saw a *bird*?" Caleb's face had gone red.

"It would have had to have been eight birds flying in a circle," Zoe pointed out calmly. "I've never seen birds do that."

"I also read that ball lighting can be a UFO," Goo went on. "A lot of scientists think they're caused by particles of silicon burning in the air. They can hover and stay around longer than regular lightning."

Jaden frowned. "But those globes of light we saw —"

"The landing lights," Caleb interrupted.

"*Maybe* landing lights," Jaden said. "Goo's right. We all jumped to a big conclusion. We don't know for sure that what we saw was an alien spacecraft. We have to consider all the possibilities." He looked over at Goo. "Could there be a group of lightning balls moving in sync the way the ones we saw did?"

Goo shook her head. "Not in the articles I found," she said.

"What other things did UFOs turn out to be?" Dylan asked.

"Meteors, satellites, Venus on the nights it's especially bright, weather balloons," Goo said, ticking off the possibilities on her fingers.

"None of the things on Goo's list would move in a group, all together," Zoe commented. "Meteors wouldn't. There's not more than one Venus. And who would want eight weather balloons in one spot?"

"So we're left with the alien spacecraft." Caleb slammed his fists on the table.

"Or something we haven't thought of yet," Jaden said. "We have to keep our minds open. We're scientists. We need more facts and more evidence."

"Maybe the UFO will come back," Sonja said hopefully. "Maybe it will leave something else behind."

"We better hope it comes back soon," Caleb muttered. "We have a competition to win."

* * *

"I can't wait. We're going to crush them!"

Zoe heard the loud voice as soon as she walked into the media center that afternoon with Caleb and Jaden. "Who is that?" she asked. "I know I've heard that voice before, but I can't remember when."

"Crush, crush, crush!" the voice continued.

Zoe stepped around the last row of bookshelves and gasped when she saw who'd been speaking — Barrett Snyder! He'd attended Hubble Middle School earlier in the year and had wanted desperately to be in S.M.A.R.T.S., but his grades hadn't been good enough. Barrett had been really mad, and his brother, Kevin, had decided to get revenge by framing the S.M.A.R.T.S. for breaking into the school and pranking the principal's car.

Thankfully, Caleb, Jaden, and Zoe had figured out the truth before it was too late.

"What are you doing here?" Caleb demanded, glaring at Barrett, who was standing in a group of eight other kids. "I thought you and your brother changed schools. And we were all happy you did."

"I'm happy I did too," Barrett snapped. "My new school is way cooler. And so is the science club."

"Yeah, he's a Mad Scientist now," said a tall girl standing nearby. "We're the best club in the state."

Before the S.M.A.R.T.S. could reply, Mr. Leavey and Mrs. Ram walked in, followed by another grown-up.

"Great! Everybody's here," Mr. Leavey said. His hair was sticking up on one side. He kept the media center neat but never managed to keep himself the same way. "Mad Scientists, meet the S.M.A.R.T.S. And S.M.A.R.T.S., meet the Mad Scientists."

"This is Mr. Olsen, the Mad Scientists' sponsor. He's also the librarian at their school," Mr. Leavey continued, gesturing to the man beside him. Mr. Olsen gave a wave.

"He, Mrs. Ram, and I are going down to the principal's office for a few minutes to finalize the plans for the competition. In the meantime, get to know each other!"

As soon as the adults left, Barrett's face transformed into a mean smirk. "You should give up now," he told the S.M.A.R.T.S. "You'll never come up with a project as cool as ours. Never."

"Yeah," one of Barrett's teammates agreed. "We saw something out of this world last night. Nothing you think of will top it."

"It was really weird," Barrett added, staring directly at Jaden. "We just looked up, and there it was! We knew right then and there that the contest was ours."

They were talking about the UFO. Jaden was sure of it. The Mad Scientists and the S.M.A.R.T.S. had both chosen the same mystery to solve!

7

"They stole our idea!" Caleb complained after the Mad Scientists had left an hour later. Mrs. Ram and Mr. Leavey were back in the librarian's office, working on more plans for the day of the competition. "We're DOOMED!"

"How did they even know about it?" Zoe asked, nibbling on a leftover cookie. "Their school is too far away for them to have seen it, and it wasn't on the news. It's like they found out we saw it and decided to copy us."

"But we don't know any of them — well, except for Barrett, and none of us talk to him," Antonio said. "So how would they have found out?"

"It doesn't matter *how* they found out, just that they did. So what are we going to do?" Sonja asked.

"We're going to keep working on the UFO," Zoe decided. "We're the S.M.A.R.T.S. That means we're smarter. And we'll prove it by doing the same project better than they could even dream about doing it."

"What are we supposed to do until the UFO shows up again?" Antonio asked.

"More research," Jaden suggested. "We need to know as much about UFOs as we can. Remember what Goo said — Unidentified Flying Object doesn't automatically equal spaceship."

Just then Sonja waved them over to the computer she was using. "You guys have to see this!" she called.

"Wow," Zoe said when they'd all gathered around the screen. "That looks just like the UFO we saw. It has that same ring of lights on the bottom."

"People saw this one flying over a baseball stadium in Vancouver," Sonja explained.

"Did they find out what it was?" Jaden asked. He wanted to gather as many facts as possible.

"The local police said they thought it was a kite with lights on it or maybe a remote-controlled toy helicopter," Sonja said. "But ours was definitely bigger. Each of the landing lights was probably as big as a kite!"

"I found an article about these sixty-two kids in Africa who saw an alien riding on top of a UFO," Zoe said. "Sixty-two kids wouldn't all agree to tell the same lie. It has to be true! Their principal even asked them to draw pictures, and they all looked the same!"

"What did they want?" Caleb asked. "Did the aliens talk to those kids? Did they do anything to them?" His voice rose with every question.

"They didn't talk, but some kids said they communicated telepathically," Zoe told him. "They told the kids that humans were destroying the planet with pollution and that there would be 'extreme and dire consequences' if we didn't change."

"What kind of extreme and dire consequences?" Caleb demanded, his voice getting even louder. "Like the aliens would come back and attack? What if that's why they're here now? We're DOOMED!"

Before anyone could answer, an oscillating whine filled the room — high, low, high, low.

"They're back!" Caleb cried.

Zoe spun toward the window. Sure enough, a circle of eight lights glowed in the darkening sky. "We have to catch them this time!" she exclaimed.

The S.M.A.R.T.S. charged toward the door. Jaden was with them this time, but when his friends headed for the front door — and the flight of steps on the other side — he powered his wheelchair in the other direction, heading for the closest exit with a ramp.

Jaden got to the meadow before the others — but it was empty. Either the UFO hadn't landed or it *had* landed and vanished, just like before. Jaden pushed the speed on his chair up as high as it would go and started toward the woods. He caught a glimpse of his friends coming around the corner of the school building, but he kept going. He was closer to the woods. Maybe he could see something.

Unfortunately, Jaden had to stop when the trees in front of him grew too dense for his chair to fit through. Before he could look for a wider path, he heard a strange sound. Not the whining from before — a flapping sound. It was kind of familiar, but he couldn't figure out why.

"We're going in, Jaden!" Zoe called to him before she disappeared between the trees. Within a few seconds, all the other kids had gone into the woods too.

Jaden decided to do a check of the meadow. Maybe there'd be something else left behind, something they could analyze. He rolled back across the grass toward the school, going at the slowest speed so he wouldn't miss anything.

The ship — if that's what it was — seemed to have landed in the same place as before. There were more tracks, although Jaden couldn't be sure how many had been made by the S.M.A.R.T.S. But there was one set of tracks heading away from the others.

Those tracks couldn't have been made by someone in S.M.A.R.T.S., Jaden realized. Both times the UFO had appeared, they'd all gone out the front entrance of the school and had entered the meadow a couple hundred feet from where he was. These tracks were heading *toward* the school.

The grass had started to spring back up, making the tracks hard to follow. Jaden gave a growl of frustration when he reached the asphalt of the back parking lot. There was no way he'd be able to keep following the tracks. Unless whoever — or whatever — he was tracking had veered over to the dirt below the windows on this side of the school.

Jaden cut over and studied the ground as he slowly moved down the side of the building. Nothing, nothing, nothing. Wait! Just then he noticed a spot where the dirt looked like it had been stepped on.

Jaden looked up and realized he was staring directly into the makerspace. Had someone been standing outside the window? Had an alien been observing them?

8

Zoe zigged around one tree, zagged around another.
The aliens had to have gone into the woods. There was
no place else they could have disappeared to so quickly.
The branches of the tree up ahead were vibrating.
Something had just passed by.

"Stop!" Zoe yelled. "We don't want to hurt you." She
really, really hoped the aliens felt the same way.

Suddenly her foot hit something slick, and Zoe
found herself flat on her back. She used both hands to

push herself up, then looked around to see what she'd slipped on — a plastic garbage bag. She picked it up. She wasn't going to leave trash in the woods. That was just wrong.

Zoe had just gotten back on her feet when she heard someone scream. That sounded like Caleb! "Caleb?" she shouted. "Are you okay? Where are you?"

"Over here!" Caleb answered. His voice was shaky.

Zoe raced in the direction of his voice and then froze. A man had caught Caleb and was holding him firmly by the arm. "Let him go!" she yelled.

"I told you kids not to come in here again!" the man said, his eyes filled with anger.

"I've never even seen you before," Caleb protested.

"Neither have I!" Zoe exclaimed, rushing over to them.

"Well, I told your friends, then." The man let go of Caleb's arm. "Look, I'm sorry I scared you, but I can't allow the *Aconitum noveboracense* to become extinct. Every plant, every insect, every living thing in these woods is part of an ecosystem. If the Monkshood disappears, who knows what might be next. At some point it might even be us, especially if we keep leaving our trash all over Mother Earth's body." He shook the

hand he hadn't been using to hold Caleb, and Zoe saw that he held some plastic straws, foil, and other garbage.

"You're one of the Flower Power people," Caleb said. "I read about you online."

"That's right," the man said. "I lead the group. You can call me Oleander. Everyone in the group has taken the name of a flower to show our commitment to the cause."

"Monkshood is on a list of endangered species," Caleb explained to Zoe. "The Red Pines Woods still have some, though."

Oleander nodded. "And I want to keep it that way," he said. "Please be careful walking out, especially if you go by the pond. They love that area. So many of them have been trampled or yanked from the earth to decorate someone's dinner table. I don't understand how anyone can eat with a dead thing a few feet away."

Caleb looked behind him to make sure he wasn't going to step on anything but dirt, then backed up a few steps. Oleander was intense.

"We'll be careful," Zoe promised. She and Caleb slowly moved away, feeling Oleander watching them until they were out of sight.

"That guy was a creepy sundae with a freaky little cherry on top," Zoe said when they reached the meadow.

"You can say that again," Caleb agreed. He checked his watch. "My mom's expecting me on the late bus. I've got to go get my stuff from the media center."

"Me too," Zoe said.

When they got back to the makerspace, the rest of the S.M.A.R.T.S. were waiting. "Anything?" Caleb asked the group.

"Nothing in the woods," Goo answered. "But Jaden found footprints outside that window." She pointed to the nearest one. "It has a perfect view of the makerspace."

"Someone has been spying on us!" Antonio announced.

"I zoomed in on the prints and got some good shots," Jaden said, holding up his phone.

"I know my sneakers, and those prints were definitely made by a pair of Fuel Injectors," Dylan said, studying the image. "All the Fuel Injectors have stars as part of the tread pattern."

"Maybe aliens have replicator devices and they made —" Benjamin started.

"— copies of the shoes to blend in," Samuel finished.

"They could even make —" Benjamin continued.

"— themselves look human," Samuel concluded.

"One could be in the room right now!" they said together.

Caleb grabbed his backpack. The idea of standing around talking to an alien who'd taken on the form of one of his friends was giving him the creeps. "I've got to head to the bus," he said.

"I have to go too," Zoe said. She pulled a balled-up trash bag out of her pocket and started to throw it away.

"Wait, where'd you get that?" Jaden asked.

"I slipped on it out in the woods," Zoe answered.

Jaden held out his hand, and Zoe handed him the thin white bag. He plucked at a piece of tape stuck to the inside of the bag. "Did anyone else find anything?" he asked. "We have to think of everything as potential evidence."

"This environmentalist guy went off on us for being in the woods," Caleb offered. "He said he'd found trash out there. I think he was holding some foil." He looked over at Zoe. "Do you remember what else?"

"A couple plastic straws," Zoe said.

"This slapped me in the face while I was running," Dylan said, holding out a long, snarled hunk of string. "It was caught on a tree branch."

"So we have a trash bag, the red wax, and the pictures of the footprints," Jaden said.

"Plus some string. And there were some straws and foil found in the woods," Caleb added.

"We have less than a week before we throw down against the Mad Scientists," Zoe said, sounding frustrated. "I wonder if they've figured out more about the UFO than we have."

"I didn't know we'd figured out *anything*," Caleb muttered.

No one said anything for a long time. Zoe wanted to give the group a pep talk, but she couldn't think of anything peppy. An assortment of trash, red wax, and pictures of footprints wasn't much to go on. Especially because they didn't know how — or even if — those things were connected to the UFO.

NERDS RULE

9

Zoe reached over and beeped the car horn, hoping it would get Kylie out of the house and into the driver's seat. Zoe was supposed to be meeting Jaden and Caleb at the city library *now*. They'd decided to spend the day doing research and brainstorming ways the wax, trash, and sneaker print could be connected to the UFO mystery.

"I still don't understand why it's necessary to get to the library at nine o'clock in the morning on a

Saturday," Kylie grumbled as she got in the car a few moments later.

"Thanks so much for driving me," Zoe told her. "You're the best sister!"

"Oh, believe me, I know it," Kylie agreed with a wink as she backed down the driveway and started down the street.

Zoe's brain flitted back and forth between the wax, the trash, and the sneaker print as Kylie drove. She just couldn't imagine how they were connected to the UFO mystery. The S.M.A.R.T.S. really needed more clues — and fast.

As they drove past her school, Zoe saw something that made her forget all about the UFO. "Stop!" she cried. "Kylie, stop!"

"What's wrong?" Kylie exclaimed, slowly pulling over to the curb and parking.

Zoe jumped out of the car and stared at the sidewalk. Slimy green footprints, coming from the direction of the meadow and moving down the sidewalk

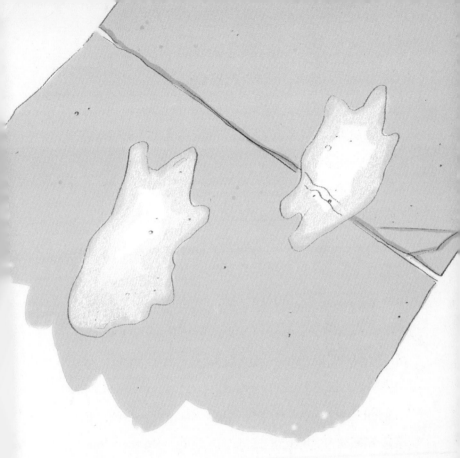

past the school, glistened in the sunlight. Zoe yanked out her cell phone and started taking pictures.

"What *are* those?" Kylie muttered when she caught up with Zoe.

"That's what I need to find out." Zoe trotted down the sidewalk, following the slimy prints. At the main entrance to the high school, the tracks turned. She followed them over to the statue of the Champ the bulldog, the high school mascot, which was covered with the same green slime.

"I can't believe someone would do that to Champ," Kylie said. "It must have been the rival high school's football team and cheerleaders. There's a big game this afternoon."

Or aliens, Zoe thought. She needed to get a sample. She rooted through her backpack until she found the little plastic bag she normally kept all her extra erasers in. She dumped the erasers out, put her hand inside the baggie, and used it to scoop up some of the slime. Then she turned the baggie inside out and sealed the slime inside.

"Why do you want that?" Kylie asked, her nose wrinkled with disgust.

"Science," Zoe told her. "Come on. I need to get to the library right away so I can show Jaden and Caleb this slime."

Kylie shook her head. "I'm glad you found some friends who are as weird as you are."

* * *

"Look at this!" Zoe exclaimed a few minutes later. She dropped the baggie of slime on the table in front of Caleb and Jaden. "There were slime footprints on the sidewalk outside our school — and they came out of the meadow!"

Jaden picked up the baggie and squeezed it between his fingers. "Maybe we should look at this under the microsc—"

"I smell nerd," Barrett interrupted loudly, stepping out from between two rows of shelves with a couple books under one arm. He wrinkled his nose like he smelled something rotten.

Zoe crossed her arms over her chest. "Best smell in the world," she shot back.

"If you're here working on your project, don't bother," Barrett told them rudely. "The Mad Scientists are almost done with ours, and there's no possible way we can lose."

"We'll see about that," Jaden told him.

Barrett rolled his eyes and shook his head. "Whatever, nerds. See you guys on Wednesday." He looked straight at Caleb. "Get ready for some extreme and dire consequences when we finally crush you."

As Barrett turned away, one of the books slid out from under his arm. Caleb picked it up. "*Fear Itself: The Psychology of Mass Hysteria*," he read aloud. He looked up at Barrett. "Sounds like what the Mad Scientists are going to be feeling after the S.M.A.R.T.S. win the competition."

Barrett grabbed the book and stalked away. When he'd disappeared from sight, Zoe asked, "Do you think Barrett was telling the truth? Have the Mad Scientists solved the UFO mystery? What are we going to do? We're not even close to a solution."

Jaden opened his mouth but then shut it. He didn't have an answer.

10

"We can't keep sitting here doing nothing," Jaden said. It had been almost thirty minutes since Barrett had left the library, and they'd gotten exactly nowhere. "Let's go over the evidence again. The answer has to be there somewhere."

"We have a new clue — the slime footprints," Zoe said. "I took some pictures. Let's start there." She pulled out her phone, but before she could hand it to the boys, a loud noise rustled behind them.

Jaden turned to see a custodian holding a trash bag. "I know that sound!" he exclaimed. "Do that again! Make that noise with the bag."

The woman looked at him like he was crazy but gave the trash bag another shake to open it up.

"Now a bunch of times in a row," Jaden said.

The woman gave the bag four shakes. "That's all I've got time for," she told him, pushing her cart of cleaning supplies toward the restrooms.

"I heard that flapping sound in the meadow right after we saw the UFO the second time!" Jaden exclaimed. "I knew I'd heard it before, but I couldn't remember where. It's from when I was cleaning my room. My dad shook a trash bag, and it made the same sound. But in the meadow it was louder, like a whole bunch of bags flapping through the air at once."

"I found that one trash bag in the woods," Zoe said.

Jaden thought for a moment. "The bag was white. If you blew it up, it might look like one of the white globes we saw."

"What we saw were landing lights," Caleb protested. "Trash bags are the right shape if they're blown up, but they don't glow like those lights did."

"The bags are really thin, though," Jaden said. "Thin enough that if there was some kind of light inside, it would shine through."

"Fine. I'll give you that. They'd look like what we saw," Caleb admitted. "If there happened to be eight of them flying in a circle. But how would eight trash bags — with lights in them — end up in that formation in the sky?"

"What if they didn't just *end up* in that formation? What if someone figured out how to light them up and fly them in a circle? What if someone faked the UFO?" Zoe said, speaking faster with every word. "My neighbor, Austin, goes all-out decorating his house for Halloween. He even does some things around town —"

"I know who you're talking about!" Jaden interrupted. "He's the guy that made it look like zombies were attacking his house a couple years ago. He even put stuff that looked like half-eaten brains around town a few weeks before Halloween, right? My mom almost puked when she saw some outside the bakery."

Zoe nodded. "Yep, that was Austin. What if this year he's going to make it look like aliens landed in his yard? What if everything we've seen is the beginning of his Halloween plan?"

Caleb picked up the baggie of slime. "It wouldn't be that hard to make slime like this for the footprints. I have this kitchen science book that tells you how to make goop out of cornstarch and water. A little green food coloring, and this could be it."

"So that's how the alien tracks were faked!" Zoe said. "But what about the other stuff?"

"Let's go over the other evidence we found," Jaden suggested. "We have a white plastic bag and a piece of wax."

"There was a piece of tape on the inside of the bag," Zoe added.

"And there were drinking straws and foil in the woods too," Caleb added. "Oleander, the guy that's trying to save the Monkshood plant, had that stuff in his hand. He said somebody had left the trash behind."

"And Dylan found string," Jaden said.

"I'm writing this down," Zoe told them.

Clues:
- Irregular disk of red wax
- White trash bag with piece of tape on it
- Foil
- Plastic straws
- String

"Oleander was in the woods right after we saw the UFO," Caleb said. "What if he's behind it? Maybe he thought it would scare people and keep them out of the woods. That would keep people away from the Monkshood."

"Okay, so we're saying someone, maybe Oleander or Austin, used trash bag balloons to fake a UFO," Zoe said. "But how were they glowing? It's not like you could put a flashlight inside. That would be too heavy. The bag wouldn't achieve liftoff."

"Even the battery for a little LED light would probably weigh too much," Caleb agreed.

"What if the light was part of the flight mechanism?" Jaden suggested. "I went to a hot air balloon festival with my parents once. When it got dark, you could see flames from the burners that produced the hot air glowing in the sky."

"Trash bags are a lot smaller than hot air balloons. Do you think a candle would give off enough heat to get one in the air?" Zoe asked. "And maybe leave a little *wax* behind?"

Jaden nodded. "Now we're on to something. It wouldn't be hard to make eight plastic bags disappear. The flapping I heard could have been someone running away while holding all the bags."

"Except the one that got dropped." Zoe grinned. Now they were getting somewhere.

"We have a hypothesis," Caleb said. "We all know what we have to do next — test it!"

11

That night, about an hour before dark, all the
S.M.A.R.T.S. gathered in the meadow beside school.
Jaden had texted everyone earlier to tell them the new
theory and plan.

"Fellow scientists," Jaden called out. "We're here to
test a hypothesis. Can a hot air balloon be made using
these materials?" He pointed to the group of objects
laid out in front of them: a box of thin plastic bags,
a roll of tape, an assortment of candles, a roll of foil,

a box of straws, and a ball of string. "If so, we'll be a lot closer to winning the competition against the Mad Scientists!"

That's all he had to say. The S.M.A.R.T.S. kids were off, assessing the supplies, making plans.

"One of us should film what we're doing," Caleb suggested. "We might want it for our presentation on Wednesday."

The group worked in silence, except for an occasional question or comment.

"I just realized what the string is for!" Goo burst out. "It's so we can fly the balloons! If we all use string that's the same length and stand in a circle, we can make a circle of balloons that will look like the UFO we saw!"

"You're right!" Sonja called. "I'll cut pieces for all of us."

While the girls cut string, Caleb taped three plastic straws together into a long plastic stick, then repeated it with three new straws. Next he took the two plastic sticks he'd made and taped them together so that they formed a cross. "Who has the foil?" he asked.

"Here!" Sonja called, tossing him the roll.

Caleb ripped off a piece and folded it until it seemed thick enough to support some candles, then he taped the foil platform to the center of the crossed plastic straws. Now he just needed to tape the four ends of the cross to the inside of a plastic bag so it would hold the bag open.

Caleb grinned as he studied his creation. "This might really work!" he exclaimed. "I think I'm ready for candles!"

Zoe came over with a box of candles left over from her dad's fiftieth birthday party. They were the trick ones that relit after they'd been blown out, which made them perfect for sending into the air. The wind wouldn't keep them out for long!

Zoe lit one of the candles, dripped some wax onto the foil, and held one of the other candles in the wax until it was stuck to the foil. "Done!"

"Me too," Jaden said. He tugged lightly on the string he'd tied to the platform holding his candles and looked around at the rest of the group. There were eight balloons ready to go. "Time to fly them. On the count of three. One! Two! Three!"

The S.M.A.R.T.S. all moved into position — where they'd originally thought the landing wheels had come to rest — and lit the candles of their small hot air balloons. There was a collective gasp as the candles shone through the thin plastic bags, turning each one into a glowing, golden orb.

Everyone slowly let the balloons rise into the darkening sky. Each one was attached to an identical piece of string, so when the balloons reached the ends of the tethers, they hovered in a circle. Antonio stood outside the circle, filming everything.

"Mine's too heavy!" Dylan moaned, as his balloon took a nosedive. "The candle I used must have been too big."

"I think my candle burned through my plastic bag!" Goo shouted as hers started falling too.

"Doesn't matter!" Caleb exclaimed, staring up at the circle of glowing orbs. "That's it! That's our UFO!"

NERDS RULE

12

"We did it! I told you the S.M.A.R.T.S. were smart enough!" Zoe said Monday at lunch. Everyone was sharing a table again. They had a lot to talk about — like how to come up with a great presentation showing how they'd solved the UFO mystery.

"We've solved *part* of it," Jaden corrected. "The *how*. What we haven't figured out is the *who*."

"It's either Zoe's neighbor or that guy Oleander. That's what you said you guys figured out in the library," Antonio said.

"They both have motive," Jaden agreed. "Austin could be behind the UFO as part of his Halloween prank, and Oleander might be trying to keep people out of the woods to protect the Monkshood. But we shouldn't jump to conclusions. Can anybody think of any other suspects?"

For a few moments everyone just chewed and thought.

"I can't think of anyone else," Sonja admitted.

"I'm out too," Dylan said. The others nodded.

"So now what?" Caleb asked.

"Now we have to figure out which of our suspects is the guilty one," Jaden answered. "And we have to get proof!"

* * *

As soon as school was let out for the day, everyone in S.M.A.R.T.S. rushed to the makerspace. They needed to come up with a strategy to figure out which of their suspects was guilty and how to get the proof they needed. There was no time to waste.

Mrs. Ram arrived a few minutes later.

"Would you mind grading papers at the front of the media center instead of back here?" Zoe asked her politely.

Mrs. Ram pressed her hand against her heart. "But I thought I was your most favorite teacher ever," she protested with a loud, fake sniffle.

"You are," Sonja reassured her. "But we have to work on our competition project, and you aren't allowed to help."

Mrs. Ram smiled. "Okay, fair enough. Yell if you need help with any equipment. That's allowed."

As soon as Mrs. Ram was out of earshot, Zoe said, "I stopped in the bathroom on my way over here. The floor had just been mopped, and I left a footprint. That's when I realized we *do* know something about our suspect — whoever it is wears Fuel Injector sneakers. Remember the footprint by the window?"

"You're right," Caleb said. "We heard that weird whining sound both times we saw the UFO. The trash bag balloons wouldn't make that sound. So our perp must have made it — right outside the window."

"We need to find out if Austin or Oleander wears Fuel Injectors," Jaden told the group. "But how?"

"This isn't a how, but you know what we should do? Make one of those plaster casts of the shoe print," Sonja suggested. "It would be great as part of our presentation for the contest."

"That's an incredible idea!" Zoe told her. "We'd be like crime scene investigators!"

"Goo, any idea how to make a plaster cast of a shoe print?" Jaden asked.

Goo nodded. "We just have to mix plaster of Paris in something like a plastic milk jug. Then we brush any debris out of the print with a paintbrush, make a little hole in the bottom of the jug, and fill up the track with the plaster of Paris a little at a time. If you just dump it on, it could destroy the print before the mold is made. Then we wait for the plaster to dry and pick it up."

"I can be on Team Plaster," Antonio volunteered.

"I'm on the team too, since I thought of it," Sonja said. The two of them headed to the makerspace supply cupboard to get started.

"So, how are we going to get our suspects' shoes to compare them with the print?" Caleb asked. "A little breaking and entering?"

"I think it would be better if we were invited in," Jaden said.

"I can't exactly see Oleander welcoming us with open arms," Zoe told him. "He was really mad when he found us in the woods."

Suddenly Caleb had a brilliant realization. "Maybe we don't have to match the print to Oleander's shoes." He looked over at Dylan. "Do you know what materials Fuel Injector sneakers are made of? Actually, all I really need to know is if any part of them is made of leather."

"Yeah, definitely," Dylan answered.

"That rules out Oleander," Caleb said. "One of the articles I read said he doesn't wear anything made from plant or animal products. He wants everything to be a man-made material, and he tries to buy stuff that's recycled."

"Case closed." Zoe clapped her hands. "That means Austin is our culprit!"

"Probably," Jaden agreed. "But we still need proof. That's what's going to win us the contest."

"Well, we're not going to get proof here," Zoe said. "I've lived next door to Austin my whole life. I'll figure out a way to get a look at his shoes. If one matches the print, we're golden."

13

That afternoon, Zoe pulled up the high school website and checked the football team's schedule. Lucky for her, Austin was on the team, and they had practice that afternoon.

Zoe breathed a sigh of relief. It would be a lot easier to get a peek into Austin's closet if Austin wasn't around. With that, she went next door, marched herself up to the Harris's front porch, and rang the bell.

A moment later, Austin's mother opened the door. "Hi, Zoe. How are you?"

"Not so good," Zoe asked, giving a sigh that she hoped didn't seem too fake. She liked Austin's mom and felt sort of bad for tricking her. "I forgot my key. Could I use your bathroom?"

"Of course. You know the way." She stepped back, letting Zoe inside.

"Thanks!" Zoe said. She hurried across the living room and down the hall. Lucky for her, there was a bathroom right across from Austin's bedroom. She shot a quick glance behind her to make sure Mrs. Harris wasn't watching, then ducked into his room.

Zoe looked around and grimaced — Austin was a super slob. There were dirty clothes everywhere — including a pair of jeans with what looked like green slime stains on them! Zoe took a picture, then looked around for sneakers. Nothing. She kicked at the piles of clothes, hoping to unearth something, but came up empty-handed.

Guess I'll have to check under the bed, Zoe thought. She stretched out on her stomach and started to feel around under the bed. Her fingers brushed against something scaly. Zoe let out an involuntary squeak and jerked her hand away. What was that?

Cautiously pressing her cheek against the floor so she could see what she'd just touched, Zoe peered under the bed. A full-size swamp monster with huge yellow

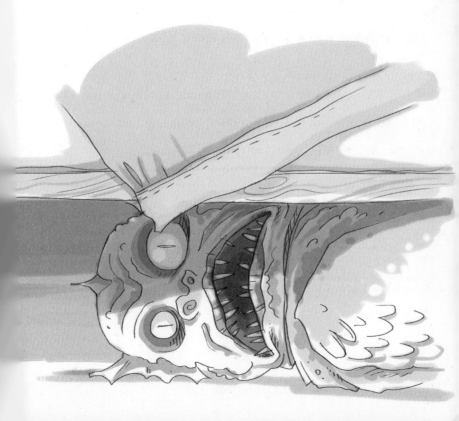

eyes stared back at her. Green fins stuck out from the side of its face and the top of its head, and its mouth was filled with dozens of needle sharp teeth.

"It's not real," Zoe said aloud aloud. "It's just for Halloween." She took a deep breath and forced herself to look past the monster. Sure enough, she spotted a Fuel Injector sneaker hiding just beyond it. She grabbed it, scrambled to her feet, jammed the shoe in her backpack, and bolted.

"Thanks, Mrs. Harris!" Zoe yelled as she went out the front door.

When she was safely back in her own house, she shot a mass text to her S.M.A.R.T.S. teammates: "Got Austin's Fuel Injector sneaker! Case (almost) solved!"

* * *

Zoe got to school early Tuesday morning. When she entered the makerspace, Jaden, Caleb, Goo, and Antonio were already there editing the video footage from Saturday when they'd made their "UFO."

Zoe plopped Austin's sneaker down in front of them. "It's kind of smelly, but I think it will be great to show the actual sneaker next to the plaster cast."

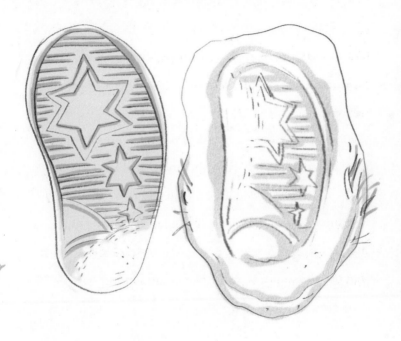

"It will," Goo agreed. She hurried to her table, grabbed the shoe print, and brought it over. She set it down next to the actual sneaker, and they all studied it.

"Uh, guys . . . it doesn't match," Caleb said.

He was right. Austin's sneaker was about a size bigger, and the print on the plaster cast showed a worn spot on the inside of the foot that Austin's sneaker didn't have. His had a worn patch on the heel.

"But I saw stains on his jeans that matched the slime from the footprints on the sidewalk," Zoe insisted. "He made those tracks. I know it. I just don't get it."

For a moment, everyone was quiet. Then Zoe realized something. "He didn't mean for them to be *alien* tracks," she said. "He meant for them to be *swamp monster* tracks. He had a huge swamp monster under his bed. It must be for his yard for Halloween. I bet the slime tracks match the swamp monster's feet." She groaned. "What are we going to do? We don't have any other suspects, and the competition is tomorrow!"

"Even if we don't figure out *who* is behind the UFO hoax, at least we've solved the mystery of what the UFO actually *was*," Antonio said, but he didn't look happy.

"But what if the Mad Scientists figured out everything?" Caleb asked. "Barrett couldn't stop bragging when we saw him at the library."

"That was just Barrett being Barrett," Zoe said. "Obnoxious is his default setting."

"I hope so. Otherwise we're going to be getting those 'extreme and dire consequences' he promised us," Caleb said.

"That's not exactly a normal thing to say," Jaden said. "Who says things like 'extreme and dire consequences' anyway?"

"Hey!" Caleb exclaimed, looking a little offended. "I do."

"But that's just because it was mentioned in that article about those kids in Africa. The aliens said there would be 'extreme and dire consequences' if humans didn't stop polluting. That's where Caleb got the expression," Goo said.

"Okay, that explains why Caleb used the words. But what about Barrett?" Jaden asked.

"He must have been spying on us!" Caleb exclaimed. "We were talking about that article right before the UFO appeared for the second time, remember? I bet Barrett was the one standing by the window. The rest of the Mad Scientists were probably flying the balloons."

"Oh! I just remembered something about when Caleb and I were talking to Oleander!" Zoe added. "He said he'd already told us — or some of our friends — to stay out of the woods. But that was the first day we'd gone in there. I bet he was talking about the Mad Scientists. They ran through the woods after they flew their balloons."

"I don't get it. Why would they fake the UFO just so they could solve it?" Jaden asked. "I can believe Barrett's a big cheater, but everyone in the Mad Scientists can't be."

"I'm not sure why they did it, but we have evidence that proves they did," Caleb insisted. "I'm sure Barrett wouldn't just come up with 'extreme and dire consequences' on his own."

"I guess we'll find out why they did it tomorrow when we present our project," Zoe said. "And they'll find out we solved the whole mystery — that they created."

14

"First of all, I'd like to give a big welcome to Mr. Olsen and the Mad Scientists!" Mr. Leavey said the next afternoon. The S.M.A.R.T.S. clapped loudly and exchanged knowing looks. No one could wait to explain how they'd solved the UFO mystery, especially the part about their competitors being behind the whole thing.

"Since we're hosting in our media center, we thought we'd let the team from Edison go first," Mrs. Ram said. "The floor is yours, Mad Scientists."

"Take it away, Barrett and Amanda!" Mr. Olsen called.

Barrett and a girl from the Mad Scientists walked up to the white board mounted on the wall opposite the windows. "Could we get the lights turned off, please?" Amanda asked.

Zoe was sitting between Caleb and Jaden. "Did you see Barrett's feet?" she whispered.

"Fuel Injectors," Caleb whispered back. "Booyah."

Barrett pressed play on a computer, and Caleb's face was immediately projected onto the board. "Alien attack!" he yelled, diving under a table. Next the film clip showed Dylan strapping on goggles and a helmet, then Antonio lurching around as he ran in a zigzag pattern, then Sonja yelling for a weapon.

All the Mad Scientists laughed. Mrs. Ram looked curious, and Mr. Leavey looked concerned.

Caleb's face appeared again. "UFO!" he shouted. The image repeated several times, then a clip of Zoe explaining why aliens had appeared to children played on the screen. It wasn't clear she was talking about kids in Africa. The way it was edited made it sound like she was talking about the S.M.A.R.T.S.

Finally, two huge words filled the screen — Mass Hysteria.

"Lights please," Amanda called, and Mrs. Ram flipped them back on.

"For our project we decided to explore one of the greatest mysteries in the world — the human mind," Barrett announced.

"We wanted to see how a group of rational students, students from a *science* club, could be convinced that they'd seen an alien spacecraft, a spacecraft that was actually built by our team," Amanda said. "What you just saw illustrates how quickly fear banishes logic."

"That's why Barrett had that book on mass hysteria at the library," Jared whispered. He couldn't wait until it was their turn to present.

"The S.M.A.R.T.S.," — Amanda paused to smirk, and Barrett snickered — "became believers in an alien visitation after one sighting, even though they didn't have one single piece of hard evidence."

She and Barrett began listing examples of mass hysteria: other UFO sightings; the Salem Witch Trials, when people believed their neighbors were truly witches; sightings in Puerto Rico of a creature called *el chupacabra* that was said to drink goat blood.

"Interesting work," Mr. Leavey said when they'd finished. "Although I'm not sure filming your subjects without their consent was appropriate."

"It was all in the name of science, and no one was hurt," Mr. Olsen said.

"I agree with Mr. Leavey, but let's put that issue aside for now and hear from the S.M.A.R.T.S.," Mrs. Ram said.

Jaden and Zoe moved to the front of the group. "It's true that a lot of us were freaked out when we saw the UFO," Jaden admitted. "But once we got over our shock, we started talking about what a UFO really is — an Unidentified Flying Object."

"And that doesn't necessarily mean an alien spacecraft," Zoe continued. "So we did what scientists do — we began to gather data. The first piece was a small sample of an unknown substance." She held up the little piece of wax and explained the tests they'd done to determine what the substance was.

Jaden talked about the rest of their evidence: the plastic bag, the flapping sound, the plastic straws and foil, and the shoe print outside the window. "We thought about the materials we found near where the UFO was spotted. That led us to our hypothesis — that a white trash bag, wax candles, foil, and plastic straws could be turned into a small hot air balloon," he explained.

At that moment, Zoe played the clip showing the S.M.A.R.T.S. creating their own UFO. She looked over at Mrs. Ram, who'd taught them about the scientific method, including forming and testing a hypothesis. Mrs. Ram gave her a thumbs-up.

Next Jaden showed photos of the UFO the S.M.A.R.T.S. had created next to the one the Mad Scientists had created. They were almost identical.

"But even after we solved the *how* part of our mystery, we still didn't know *who* was behind it," Zoe told the group.

A lot of the Mad Scientists were starting to look uncomfortable. Barrett kept shifting in his chair, and Amanda was chewing on the end of her braid.

"We came up with motives for two suspects: a high school boy named Austin Harris and a man named Oleander," Jaden explained. "Austin always does Halloween decorations that extend through the town, and we thought the UFO might be part of that. Oleander is the leader of a group called the Flower Power Patrol. We thought he might have created the UFO to scare people away from the woods and protect endangered plants growing there."

Zoe nodded. "But we were able to eliminate both suspects by using a shoe print we found outside one of the media center windows," she explained. "The print didn't match shoes belonging to either Austin or Oleander."

"It was Barrett who gave us the clue we needed to finally solve the mystery," Jaden said. "Accidentally, of course. We ran into him at the library, and he used the words 'extreme and dire consequences.' It was a phrase out of an article we'd been discussing here in the makerspace. That led us to realize that the Mad Scientists had been spying on us."

Amanda whacked Barrett on the shoulder, and a couple of the Mad Scientists glared angrily in his direction.

"To finish up our presentation, we'd like to show our last bit of proof. Barrett, can we borrow your right shoe?" Jaden asked.

Barrett glared at him, but he took his shoe off and brought it up to Jaden, who turned it so the group could see the tread, then picked up the plaster cast of the shoe print.

"Identical," Jaden said. "Same size, same tread pattern, even the same worn edge."

"We also saw Barrett with a book on mass hysteria, but truthfully, we didn't realize the Mad Scientists' motive for faking the UFO until we saw their presentation," Zoe concluded. "And that is how we solved the mystery of the missing UFO."

The rest of the S.M.A.R.T.S. clapped as Zoe and Jaden returned to their seats. Mrs. Ram, Mr. Leavey, and Mr. Olsen talked for a few minutes, then stepped in front of the kids.

"We found both projects very interesting," Mr. Olsen began, "and were very impressed by the UFOs both teams made. But while we agree the brain is a fascinating mystery to study, we've decided the S.M.A.R.T.S. project was stronger. They discovered everything about the UFO, from what it was made of to who was responsible for it. Even when faced with something that could have caused hysteria, they remained scientists. Let's see if they can do it again next year, because we've decided to make the competition an annual event!"

"Woo-hoo!" Zoe cheered. She couldn't wait for another chance to go head-to-head — make that brain-to-brain — against the Mad Scientists.

"Now it's time for a saucer-shaped item I think you'll all easily identify," Mrs. Ram said. "Pizza! Everybody down to the cafeteria."

Zoe, Jaden, Caleb and the rest of the S.M.A.R.T.S. started for the door. "Congratulations, you guys," Amanda said, joining them.

"Thanks," Zoe and Caleb answered.

"You came up with an awesome way to create a UFO," Jaden added.

Barrett scowled at them. "Wait until next year," he muttered. "You think solving the mystery of a vanishing UFO was hard? Just wait."

"Bring it on," Caleb told him. "The S.M.A.R.T.S. are always ready to solve a mystery."

About the Author

Melinda Metz is the author of more than sixty
books for teens and kids, including *Echoes* and the
young adult series Roswell High, the basis of the
TV show *Roswell*. Her middle-grade mystery *Wright
and Wong: Case of the Nana-Napper* (co-authored by
the fabulous Laura J. Burns) was a juvenile Edgar
finalist. Melinda lives in Concord, North Carolina,
with her dog, Scully, a pen-eater just like the dog who
came before her.

About the Illustrator

Heath McKenzie is a best-selling author and illustrator
from Melbourne, Australia. Over the course of his
career, he has illustrated numerous books, magazines,
newspapers, and even live television. As a child, Heath
was often inventing things, although his inventions
didn't always work out as planned. His inventions still
only work some of the time . . . but that's the fun of
experimenting!

Glossary

analyze (AN-uh-lize) — to study something very closely and carefully, often by examining its individual parts

ball lightning (BAWL LITE-ning) — a rare, round type of lightning which appears during thunderstorms; it can be as small as a pea or several meters in diameter

brittle (BRIT-uhl) — easily broken or snapped

dire (DIRE) — terrible and causing great fear and worry

endangered (en-DAYN-jurd) — close to becoming extinct

hypothesis (hye-POTH-uh-siss) — a temporary prediction that can be tested

hysteria (hi-STER-ee-uh) — a state in which a person's emotions, such as fear, cause them to act in a wild, uncontrolled way

imprint (IM-print) — a mark made by pressing something into a surface

motive (MOH-tiv) — the reason why a person did something

oscillate (OS-uh-late) — to move back and forth regularly

potential (puh-TEN-shuhl) — possible but not actual or real yet

property (PROP-ur-tee) — a defining characteristic or quality of something

seismic (SIZE-mik) — relating to or caused by an earthquake

terrain (tuh-RAYN) — a piece of land

Discussion Questions

1. What unexplained mystery would you like to solve? How would you investigate the mystery? Discus some different possibilities.

2. Sometimes being scared or nervous can affect how we think, so it's good to know how to calm down and think clearly. Talk about ways you calm yourself when you're nervous.

3. While you were reading, did you ever suspect that the Mad Scientists were behind the UFO? Discuss why or why not.

Writing Prompts

1. Mrs. Ram and Mr. Leavey didn't think that the Mad Scientists' project was appropriate, but Mr. Olsen disagreed. What do you think? Write a few paragraphs explaining why it was or was not a good project.

2. When the S.M.A.R.T.S. slowed down to think about all the possibilities, they were able to discover the truth behind the UFO mystery. List ways that slowing down and taking your time can help you think through a problem.

3. S.M.A.R.T.S. is a great group for kids interested in science, engineering, and problem solving. Write about a group that you would like to form for kids interested in a certain subject. What would you call your group? What would you do during meetings?

UFOs

The modern UFO craze began in 1947, when
Kenneth Arnold saw what reports described as "flying
saucers" near Mount Rainier in Washington. After
that sighting, more and more people reported seeing
strange objects in the sky, so the United States Air
Force began investigating. But instead of calling the
objects flying saucers, in 1953 they started calling
them Unidentified Flying Objects, or UFOs for short.
Investigations like Project Blue Book, which lasted
from 1952 to 1969, explained more than ninety
percent of the sightings. Although there were still
some unexplained cases, the United States government
concluded that further study was no longer necessary.

Nowadays, many people use the term UFO to refer
to alien spacecrafts. But what might first look like
an unidentified object can usually be identified and

explained. Sometimes it's a bright star, planet, or meteor. Sometimes it's a military aircraft or weather balloon. Other times it's a deliberate hoax.

Although many scientists don't take UFO sightings very seriously, there are some groups who still investigate the claims and collect information on the sightings. Groups like Center for the Study of Extraterrestrial Intelligence and Center for UFO Studies search for proof of extraterrestrial life visiting Earth.

Even if most scientists don't believe that UFOs are proof of aliens coming to Earth, many believe it's possible that there is life somewhere in space. A lot of research goes into looking for evidence of any life beyond our planet, whether that life is a whole civilization or tiny microorganisms.

More adventure and science mysteries!

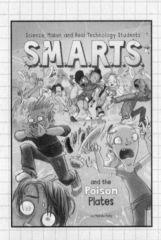
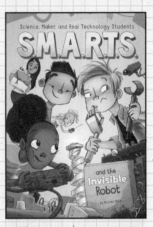

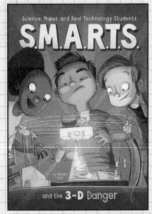